NELLIE

A Cat on Her Own

IS FOR

PETER SARGENT FRATTAROLI

MY FIRST GRANDCHILD

STORY AND PICTURES

BY *Natalie Babbitt*

A SUNBURST BOOK

FARRAR, STRAUS AND GIROUX

NELLIE

A Cat on Her Own

There was a little marionette once, named Nellie, who hung from a comfortable peg in the cottage of a clever old woman.

The old woman had made Nellie from wood and yarn and broom straws, and every afternoon would take her down from her peg, wind up the music box, and pull her strings to make her leap and dip and spin, just like a dancer on a stage.

There was a real cat living in the cottage, too. The old woman called him Big Tom. But he didn't belong to her, as Nellie did. He belonged only to himself. Still, he liked a warm fire and a bowl of milk, and so he stayed. And every afternoon he would watch in a puzzled way while Nellie danced.

One night, when the old woman was asleep, Big Tom said to Nellie, "It would be better if you danced all on your own."

"I could never do that," said Nellie.

"Moonshine!" said Big Tom. And he sprang up to the window and went out into the dark, as he always did, to go wherever it is cats go and do whatever they do.

Nellie stayed behind, as she always did. She never wondered where it was that Big Tom went or what he did. She was much too busy thinking how lovely it would be when she could dance again.

It was a safe little life for Nellie, but then one day the old woman, who was very, very old, fell sick, and after a time she died. Her friends all came and took her away to the church-yard, and Nellie and Big Tom were left alone.

"Whatever shall I do," wailed Nellie, "without my clever old woman?"

"The thing to do," said Big Tom, "is go on to the next old woman."

"But I belonged to this old woman," said Nellie. "I don't want another."

"Belong to yourself, then, like me," said Big Tom. "That way, when changes come, you'll always be ready to hold your tail high and move along."

"I can't hold my tail high and move along," said Nellie. "I can't dance, either – not without my clever old woman. And you have no idea how lovely it is to dance."

"Moonshine!" said Big Tom. "Still, you mustn't stay here. You'd better come with me." And he began to pull off the strings that were fastened to Nellie.

"Oh!" cried Nellie. "Don't take away my strings!"

"If I don't," said Big Tom, "they'll get in the way and tangle up." And he went on pulling till at last Nellie dropped to the floor with a *clunk*. "There," he said. "You're free."

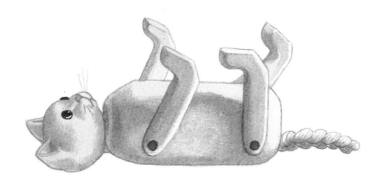

He picked her up by the leg, ignoring her squeaks and squeals, and jumped with her through the window. Then he fetched the old woman's hat and sat Nellie up inside it. "Here is your cart," he said, "and I'll be your pony." And he took the hat's long ribbons in his mouth and dragged it off, Nellie and all, into the wide, wild world.

Nellie had never once been out in the world before. It made her feel small, and at last she said again, "Whatever shall I do?" But Big Tom paid no attention.

They had not gone far when down from a tree leaned a cat with stripes. "Well!" he said. "Who's this you've got here?"

"It's Nellie," said Big Tom. "We're moving."

"But you'll be there tonight?" asked the cat with stripes.

"Oh, yes," said Big Tom. "It's right on our way."

"Good," said the cat with stripes, and he settled back into the tree.

As they started on, Nellie said, "I didn't know there were other cats."

"Moonshine!" said Big Tom.

"But what did he mean about tonight?" asked Nellie.

"There's a gathering," said Big Tom. "A gathering of friends."

For a while, as she bumped along, Nellie thought about what a gathering might be. It sounded risky, especially without her clever old woman, and she was just wishing she were back in the cottage, hanging from her peg, when out from the weeds slipped a cat as black as chimney soot. "There you are," he said. "And who might this child be?"

"It's Nellie," said Big Tom. "We're moving."

"But you'll be with us later?" asked the black cat.

"Yes, indeed," said Big Tom.

"Good," said the black cat. "Bring Nellie." And he slipped away again into the weeds.

When he was gone, Nellie said, "Another cat!"

"You'll see them all tonight," said Big Tom.

"And I can watch what you do?" asked Nellie.

"You'll do it with us, I expect," said Big Tom.

Nellie was surprised to hear this. But she began to think that, whatever happened at a gathering, it might be rather nice to be one of the friends who gathered.

They came soon after to the foot of a little hill and started up, just as the day was dimming to a close.

"I've never been off my peg so late before," said Nellie.

"You'll like it," said Big Tom.

When they came to the top of the hill, Big Tom said, "This is the place. We're just in time."

And then the moon swam up, round and full.

"Oh my!" said Nellie.

"Yes," said Big Tom. "I knew you'd like it."

Out from the shadows, the cats began to gather. One of them started to sing, and then they were all singing, and all began to dance in the moonlight.

"Oh my!" said Nellie.

Up rose Big Tom on his strong hind legs and bowed to Nellie. "Would you care to dance?" he asked her.

Nellie felt a stirring in her wooden limbs, and she stood up tall in the old woman's hat and stepped out over the brim.

"I somehow thought you could," said Big Tom, "at a gathering."

"Is it magic?" whispered Nellie.

And Big Tom answered, "Moonshine, mostly."

Then he took her paw in his, and she leapt and dipped and spun, like a dancer on a stage, and the cats all danced around her.

They danced and sang till moonset, and then the others said goodbye and went away. But Nellie and Big Tom stayed behind to watch the sun come up.

"Now," said Big Tom, "down the other side of this hill is a new old woman's cottage. Shall I take you with me?"

"I thank you very much," said Nellie, "but I do believe this is the place for me. I want to make my home here."

"Suit yourself, then," said Big Tom. But Nellie could see that he was pleased.

"Will you come and visit me?" she asked.

"Of course," said Big Tom. "I'll see you often."

So he left her in a comfortable hollow tree with a fine view of the wide, wild world, and he moved along with his tail held high.

Nellie stayed in the tree, and though she never forgot her clever old woman, she was happy and content. And every night when the moon was full, there was a gathering of friends. Big Tom would come, and Nellie danced with him. But most of the time she danced all on her own.